D1587447

Dear Parent:
Your child's love of reading starts here!

Every child learns to read in a different way and at his or her own speed. Some go back and forth between reading levels and read favorite books again and again. Others read through each level in order. You can help your young reader improve and become more confident by encouraging his or her own interests and abilities. From books your child reads with you to the first books he or she reads alone, there are I Can Read Books for every stage of reading:

SHARED READING
Basic language, word repetition, and whimsical illustrations, ideal for sharing with your emergent reader

BEGINNING READING
Short sentences, familiar words, and simple concepts for children eager to read on their own

READING WITH HELP
Engaging stories, longer sentences, and language play for developing readers

READING ALONE
Complex plots, challenging vocabulary, and high-interest topics for the independent reader

ADVANCED READING
Short paragraphs, chapters, and exciting themes for the perfect bridge to chapter books

I Can Read Books have introduced children to the joy of reading since 1957. Featuring award-winning authors and illustrators and a fabulous cast of beloved characters, I Can Read Books set the standard for beginning readers.

A lifetime of discovery begins with the magical words "I Can Read!"

*Visit www.icanread.com for information
on enriching your child's reading experience.*

Batman: Meet the Super Heroes
BATMAN, SUPERMAN, WONDER WOMAN, and all related characters and elements are trademarks of DC Comics © 2010. All
rights reserved. Manufactured in the U.S.A. No part of this book may be used or reproduced in any manner whatsoever
without written permission except in the case of brief quotations embodied in critical articles and reviews. For information address
HarperCollins Children's Books, a division of HarperCollins Publishers, 195 Broadway, New York, NY 10007.
www.icanread.com

Library of Congress catalog card number: 2009934071
ISBN 978-0-06-187858-9
Book design by John Sazaklis

17 18 19 20 LSCC 30 29 28 27 26 25 24   ❖   First Edition

I Can Read!

READING 2 WITH HELP

BATMAN™

Meet the Super Heroes

by Michael Teitelbaum
pictures by Steven E. Gordon

BATMAN created by Bob Kane
SUPERMAN created by Jerry Siegel and Joe Shuster
WONDER WOMAN created by William Moulton Marston

HARPER
An Imprint of HarperCollinsPublishers

BRUCE WAYNE

Bruce Wayne is a very rich man. He is secretly Batman.

CLARK KENT

Clark Kent is a newspaper reporter. He is secretly Superman.

DIANA PRINCE

Diana Prince works for the US government. She is secretly Wonder Woman.

BATMAN

Batman fights crime in Gotham City. He wears a mask and a cape.

SUPERMAN

Superman has many amazing powers. He was born on the planet Krypton.

WONDER WOMAN

Wonder Woman is an Amazon princess. She is very strong and has a magic lasso.

The Gotham City Museum was having a big party. Bruce Wayne was invited.

Bruce spotted a statue of a dragon.

"That's an interesting statue," he said.

Bruce had never seen anything

like it before.

Suddenly, the dragon statue came to life.

It flew into the air and shot fire from its mouth.

People screamed and ran.

"How did this happen?"

Bruce said as he ran outside.

"I've got to stop that dragon!"

Bruce rushed to his big house.

Bruce had a secret.

Bruce Wayne was Batman!

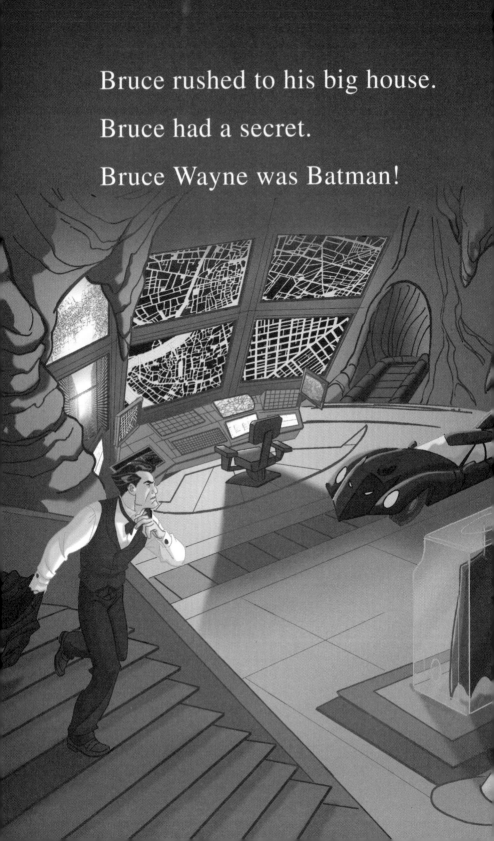

Batman raced back to the museum

in the Batmobile.

The dragon flew over the city.

Gotham was in danger!

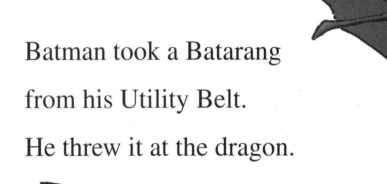

Batman took a Batarang
from his Utility Belt.
He threw it at the dragon.

The Batarang was hooked to a rope.

The rope wrapped around the dragon.

"Now I've got you!" Batman said.

The dragon bit through the rope

with large, sharp teeth.

Then it swatted Batman away

with its tail.

The dragon was too strong for Batman.

"I can't stop it alone!" Batman said.

"I have to call for help!"

Batman grabbed his sonic-wave device.

It gave off a high-pitched sound.

Only one man could hear it.

At the Daily Planet building,
Clark Kent's super-hearing
picked up the signal.
"Batman is in trouble," Clark said.

"This is a job for Superman!"

Clark changed into his costume.

"I'll have to fly at super-speed

to get to Gotham in time," he said.

Superman got to Gotham

a few minutes later.

"Batman, what happened?" he asked.

"I'm not sure," Batman said.

"But that dragon is dangerous!"

"I'll use my super-strength
to stop that dragon,"
Superman said.

Superman flew up to the dragon
and grabbed its tail.

The dragon shot a blast of fire
at Superman.

"The dragon must have been
brought to life by magic,"
Superman said.

"My powers can't stop magic,
but Diana's can," he said.

In Washington, DC,

Diana Prince's phone rang.

It was Batman.

"I'll be right there," Diana said,

"as Wonder Woman!"

Wonder Woman took off
in her Invisible Jet.
"Statues don't just come alive
and breathe fire," she said.
"This sounds like evil magic!"

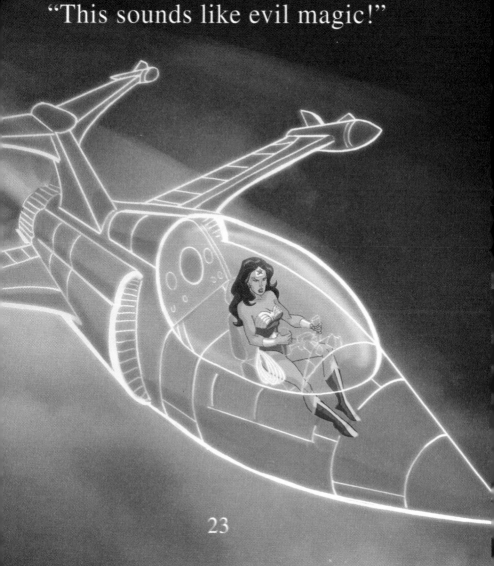

A few minutes later,

Wonder Woman joined her friends

in Gotham City.

"I have a plan," Batman said.

He explained it to the heroes.

Superman and Wonder Woman

sprang into action.

Batman got out his steel Bat-cable.

Wonder Woman threw her magic lasso
around the dragon's jaw.
It weakened the dragon.
Batman used his steel Bat-cable
to pull it to the ground.

Superman used his freezing breath
to hold the dragon.

"That should cool you off,"

he said.

"Now what?" Batman asked.

"I can link minds with the dragon,"
Wonder Woman said.

"I can try to get the dragon
to reject the evil magic."
Wonder Woman reached into
the dragon's mind.

Then the dragon vanished
in a puff of smoke.

Batman, Superman, and Wonder Woman rushed into the museum.

The dragon was once again a statue.

Batman's plan had worked!

"Nice teamwork!" he said.

"Thanks to you two,

Gotham is safe again,"

Batman said.

"Thanks to us all!" said his friends.